Rainbow Rangers™

To the Rescue

Imprint
MAKE YOUR MARK
NEW YORK

IN THE KALEIDOCOVE,

the Rainbow Rangers were hanging out between missions.

"Just try it, Floof," Anna Banana said.

"**FLOOF**," the Prismacorn said. He closed his eyes and rainbow bubbles came out of his horn.

"See? I taught him a new trick," Anna said.

"Splendiferous," Lavender LaViolette cheered.

An alert sounded. "Kalia needs us!"
Rosie Redd cried, "RANGERS GO!"

Rosie Redd— Strength Power

Mandarin Orange— Music Power

Anna Banana—Animal Power

Pepper Mintz—Inviso Power

The seven
RAINBOW RANGERS
raced to the Crystal Command Center. They activated their powers as they went.

Bonnie Blueberry— Vision Power

Lavender LaViolette—
Micro Power

Indigo Allfruit—Speed Power

Kalia waited in the Crystal Command Center. She was the leader of the Rangers, and she had a big mission for them.

A baby polar bear had floated away from his mother and needed help.

On the Mirror of Marvels, the Rangers could see the bear floating out to sea.

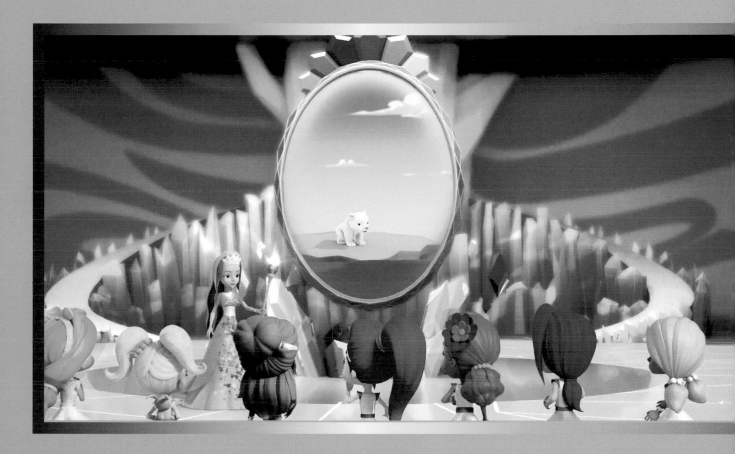

"The poor little baby bear!" Anna cried. "Kalia, what happened?"

"His ice floe in the Arctic Circle broke away," Kalia said. "He needs to be rescued, and I know just who to send."

Kalia chose Rosie, Anna, and Bonnie for the mission. They climbed on their Spectra-Scooters, and Floof hopped on Rosie's. "Ride, Rangers, ride!" Kalia called.

One rainbow-ride later, the three girls and Floof arrived at the Arctic Circle.

"I see him!" Bonnie said. Up ahead was the polar bear cub.

But far, far away was Mama Bear, high up on an ice shelf.

"It's so sad I could cry!" Anna said.

"No tears on a rescue," Rosie said. "I'll get the cub back to Mama Bear."

"Rosie, wait!" Bonnie said.

But Rosie was already zooming her Spectra-Scooter toward the bear cub.

"Take the controls," Rosie told Floof.

"**FLOOF?**" he asked. He nervously started flying the scooter. Rosie reached down and scooped up the bear cub.

But the bear cub was frightened. His wriggling made Floof lose control of the scooter.

"Rosie, you have to stop!" Anna cried.

"Not giving up!" Rosie shouted.

But the scooter rolled over.
"**JUMP!**" Rosie cried.

Rosie, the bear cub, and Floof jumped off and landed on an ice floe.

The scooter splashed down nearby.

After catching her breath, Rosie said, "That was something! Ready to try again?"

"No!" Anna shouted as she and Bonnie landed their scooters. Anna picked up the frightened bear cub. "He needs a break," Anna said.

There was a loud crack as a piece of the ice floe fell into the water.

"Why did that happen?" Anna asked. "We were just sitting here."

"It wasn't you," Bonnie said. "It was the hot sun. When temperatures get hotter, ice shelves break apart."

The bear cub cried out and held Anna tighter.

"He's too afraid to leave the ice," Anna said.

"All right," Rosie said. "If the bear won't leave the ice, the ice will come with the bear."

Working together, the Rangers used their scooters to tow the ice floe. Rosie, Bonnie, and Floof drove, while Anna stayed with the bear cub.

"Ride, Rangers, ride!" Rosie cried.

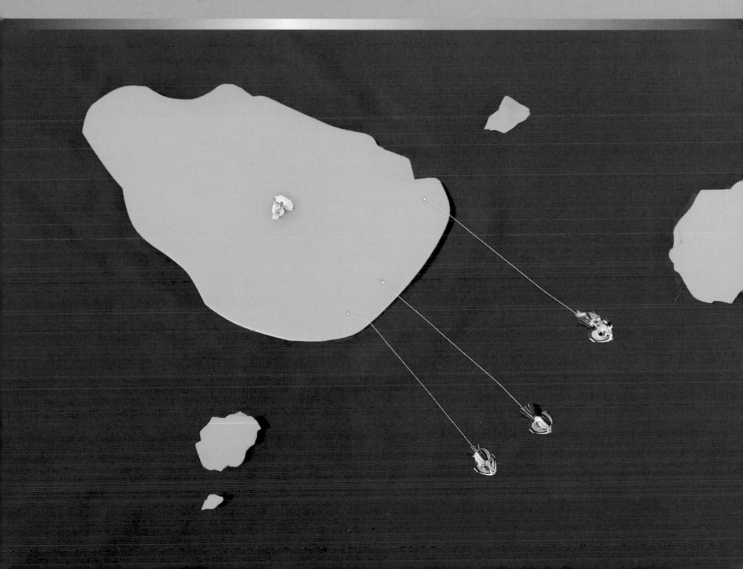

Bonnie used her Vision Power.
"Iceberg, dead ahead!"
"Hard right!" Rosie shouted.
The Rangers drove their
scooters away from the iceberg,
but Floof turned toward it.

"Your other right, Floof!" Rosie cried.

"Floof!" the Prismacorn said. He turned right just in time.

"We did it!" Anna said.

The Rangers pulled the ice floe up where Mama
Bear waited. She and the bear cub ran to each other
and cuddled happily.

"I'm happy he's home," Anna said. She looked sad.
"I'll just miss him."

The bear cub ran back to say goodbye to Anna.
"Aw," Anna said. "I love you too, baby bear."
"Mission accomplished, Rangers!" Rosie said.

The Rangers hopped on their scooters and flew off into a rainbow window in the sky. They sang out, "When trouble comes, we're on the way . . . Rainbow Rangers save the day!"

"FLOOF!"